Shopkins™

Once you shop...You can't stop!

A SURPRISE FOR SANTA!

Autumn Publishing

Christmas was coming and the Shopkins were so excited. Apple Blossom was in charge of decorating all of the shops in Shopville, so she called a meeting to give each of her friends a special job to do.

Chrissy Present couldn't wait to get started.
"I love this time of year!" she said. What will my job be?"
"Well," said Apple Blossom, thinking. "First we should
choose which shop to turn into Santa's workshop."

They all agreed the ice cream shop would be the best place in Shopville to have Santa's workshop. "It's super-chilled, plus people don't buy much ice cream at Christmas time," giggled Poppy Cracker.

Chrissy Present was even more excited now. "How can I help?" she asked again.

"Your job comes later!" Apple Blossom replied with a smile. "Now, what's next on our list?"

"Ah, yes!" said Apple Blossom remembering. "We need to let everyone know that the ice cream shop has a brand new name for Christmas." "That's a job for me!" called Lippy Lips.

In her very best handwriting, Lippy Lips
carefully wrote out SANTA'S WORKSHOP in big,
bright red letters on the ice cream shop window.
"That looks great!" the Shopkins cheered.

"Next, we need to show that Santa's workshop is in a snowy forest," said Apple Blossom. "Does anyone have any good ideas about what we can use for snow?"

"How about lots of white frosting?" said Patty Cake, who was topped with lots of white frosting herself. "Or lots of icing sugar?" said Macca Roon, who was dusted with icing sugar.

Apple Blossom was worried that using frosting and icing would be too sticky and messy. "Does anyone else have an idea?"

"Er, I do," said Sammy Santa Hat shyly.
"We could put white furry blankets on the floor."
"That's a brilliant idea!" said Apple Blossom happily.
Everyone quickly found blankets to lay down.

"Hey, Sneaky Wedge," called Snugg Ugg.
"We should make Santa's footprints in the snow!"
Together they stomped and stamped, making it look
as if Santa had walked to the workshop.

"The snow looks great," cried Apple Blossom. "But how are we going to show that Santa's workshop is deep inside a forest?"

"That's where I can help," called Teresa Tree, as she stood in the middle of the white blankets.

Teresa Tree stretched out high and wide.
"If I stand tall and spread my branches as far as
I can, it will look as if there is a whole forest of trees
right outside Santa's workshop," she explained.
"That's tree-mendous!" agreed Apple Blossom.

Their next job was to decorate Santa's workshop. "Let's start with the outside," suggested Apple Blossom. She scratched her head, wondering exactly what Santa's workshop should look like. She had no idea!

Just then, Apple Blossom saw Ginger Fred.
"Of course," cried Apple Blossom. "Santa's workshop
should be decorated just like a gingerbread house.
Everyone, let's copy Ginger Fred!"

The Shopkins had a fantastically festive time singing carols and decorating Santa's workshop. Soon it was red, green and very Christmassy!

"The workshop looks just like Ginger Fred now," said Holly Wreath, as she jumped onto the door. "Only it's a lot bigger," she said, giggling.

Next, it was time to decorate inside.
"Santa's workshop would be full of gifts, ready
to be delivered on Christmas Eve," said Wild Carrot.
"Hmm, I wonder what we could use instead?"

Ornament Annie noticed some old cardboard boxes stacked up in the corner. "How about this pile of boxes?" she said eagerly. "We could cover them in wrapping paper."

Apple Blossom looked around, wondering what else would be found inside Santa's workshop. "That's it!" she said. "Santa needs a cosy log fire, too." The Shopkins quickly used old cardboard rolls and crinkly card to make a pretend fire.

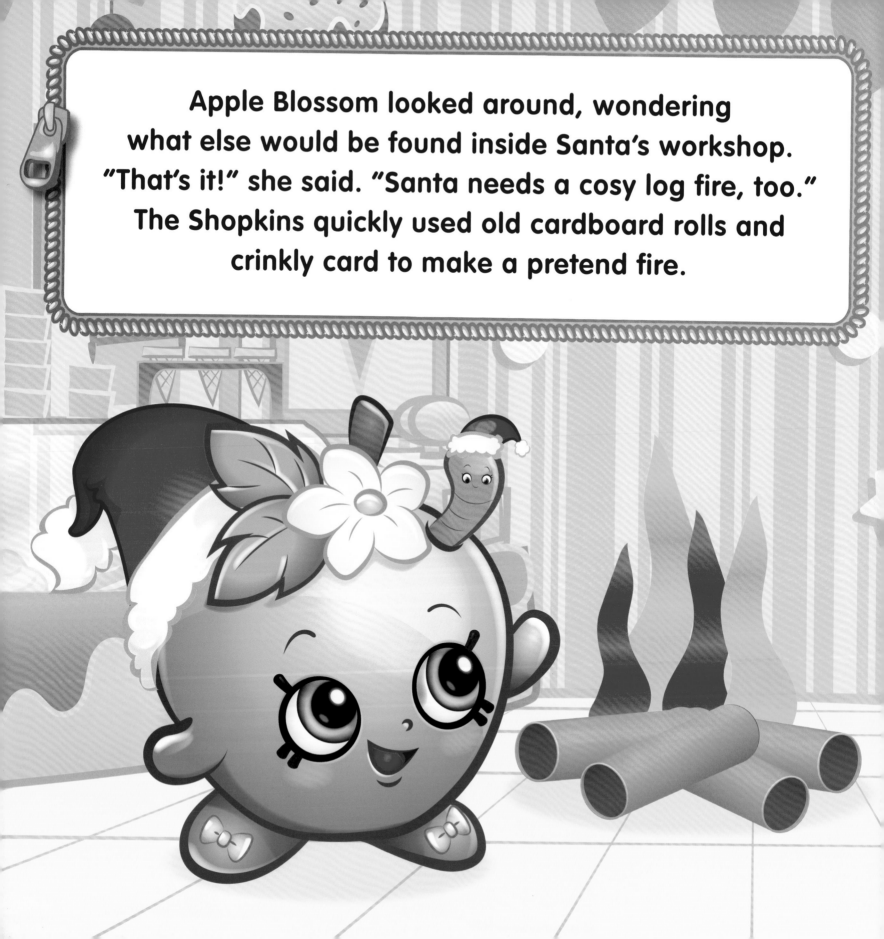

"I'll sit on a chair next to the fire," said Sammy Santa Hat. "So it looks as if Santa left his hat there to keep it warm."

"You always pick the easiest jobs, Sammy!" Patty Cake laughed.

With all the decorating finished, the Shopkins agreed they had made a wonderful workshop for Santa. Apple Blossom was delighted, but Chrissy Present wasn't quite so happy. "You didn't give me a job," she sniffed. "Did you forget all about me, Apple Blossom?"

"Not at all," chuckled Apple Blossom. "You actually have the best job. I would like you and Poppy Cracker to be two of the presents hidden inside Santa's sack ready to be delivered." Chrissy Present lit up. "That IS the best job, Apple!"

Rub the stickers to release the delicious scent!

HAPPY HOLIDAYS

HAPPY HOLIDAYS

♡spk

♡spk

MERRY CHRISTMAS